My Teacher's Not Here!

To my dearest friend, and everyone's
favorite teacher, Mr. Worrell — L.B.

To Marc, my love, my best friend and my
crazy-but-wonderful bike coach — C.B.

Kids Can Press gratefully acknowledges the financial support of the Government of Ontario, through the Ontario Media Development Corporation; the Ontario Arts Council; the Canada Council for the Arts; and the Government of Canada, through the CBF, for our publishing activity.

Published in Canada and the U.S. by Kids Can Press Ltd.
25 Dockside Drive, Toronto, ON M5A 0B5

Kids Can Press is a Corus Entertainment Inc. company

www.kidscanpress.com

The artwork in this book was rendered by hand-drawing and digital collage.
The text is set in Cabrito Didone.

Edited by Jennifer Stokes
Designed by Karen Powers

Printed and bound in Malaysia in 8/2017 by Tien Wah Press (Pte) Ltd.

CM 18 0 9 8 7 6 5 4 3 2 1

FSC
www.fsc.org
MIX
Paper from responsible sources
FSC® C012700

Library and Archives Canada Cataloguing in Publication

Button, Lana, 1968–, author
    My teacher's not here! / written by Lana Button ; & illustrated by Christine Battuz.

ISBN 978-1-77138-356-1 (hardcover)

    I. Battuz, Christine, illustrator II. Title. III. Title: My teacher is not here!

PS8603.U87M98 2018   jC813'.6   C2017-903213-5

My Teacher's Not Here!

Written by Lana Button *& Illustrated by* Christine Battuz

KIDS CAN PRESS

THERE'S TROUBLE AT SCHOOL! I can tell right away.

Miss Seabrooke? Where are you? Are you HERE today?!

Smiling Miss Seabrooke should be here to meet me.

But my teacher is missing and NOT here to greet me.

She's been coughing a lot.
Could she have the FLU?
If my teacher is sick,
we should all go home, too.

Call back those buses!
Close school for today!
Wait! Why's the BELL ringing?
Do we start ANYWAY?!

I'm brave about school —
when Miss Seabrooke is near.
How does school work
when your teacher's not here?

My Thermos gets stuck;
only SHE knows the trick.
I'll starve in my seat
while my teacher's home sick!

This jacket won't zip,
but SHE knows where to tug.
And like magic she's there
when I need a big hug.

There's no time to run,
and there's nowhere to hide.
The line starts to move,
and we're heading inside.

This class NEEDS Miss Seabrooke —
her songs and her rhymes,
her gentle reminders about ...
BATHROOM TIME!

When she LOOKS this one LOOK,
silly kids straighten up.
And when SHE flicks the lights,
EVERYONE tidies up.

I'm doing my best to keep my eyes dry
as I peek in our classroom ...
HEY!
Who is THAT guy?!

Someone is standing
in MY teacher's spot.
He's ginormously TALL.
Miss Seabrooke is not.

He's saying "good morning"
with a voice that's MUCH deeper
than the voice that comes out of
my regular teacher.

He points to a message
and asks us to look ...
Hey, I know that writing!
It's from Miss Seabrooke!

Good morning, dear children,
I'm not well today.
Mr. Omar will teach you
while I am away.

Please help Mr. Omar
however you can.
Be there for one another
and lend a kind hand.

Love, from Miss Seabrooke.
P.S. See you soon!

Then we all feel her
WONDERFUL SMILE
fill the room.

My teacher is sure I can
get through this day.
And she asked for my help ...
so I guess I should stay.

I take a deep breath
and try hard not to fuss.
How can I?
Miss Seabrooke is COUNTING on us.

Mr. Omar's not sure of
our Good Morning song.
So I SING out the words ...
then the class joins along.

I point to the things
Mr. Omar can't find
and show him our list
of who leads us in line.

I help flick the lights
so we tidy our room,
and hint to some kids
so they'll use the bathroom.

When I get to those things
that I can't do myself,
I look for a friend ...
and I ask them for help.

My Thermos unsticks
thanks to Gertie's strong grip.
And with two yanks from Yancy,
my jacket is zipped.

Miss Seabrooke just KNEW
that we'd miss her today,
so she left Mr. Omar
some fun plans for play.

He comes in handy
when stacking a tower,
and knows how to
fluff tissue into a flower.

When it's time to read stories,
he makes a good choice.
And he sings a good song
(even with that deep voice).

It's an end-of-day rush
matching kids with their things.
But we're ready for home
when the final bell rings.

The school bus is here!
I made it! I'm done!
I survived the WHOLE day.
(I even had FUN.)

This card's for my teacher,
to show her my day
and tell her I missed her
while she was away.

It's a school day tomorrow.
But before my bag's packed,
can't someone please tell me ...

WILL MY TEACHER BE BACK?